Dear Parent:
Your child's love of reading starts here!

Every child learns to read in a different way and at his or her own speed. Some go back and forth between reading levels and read favorite books again and again. Others read through each level in order. You can help your young reader improve and become more confident by encouraging his or her own interests and abilities. From books your child reads with you to the first books he or she reads alone, there are I Can Read Books for every stage of reading:

SHARED READING
Basic language, word repetition, and whimsical illustrations, ideal for sharing with your emergent reader

BEGINNING READING
Short sentences, familiar words, and simple concepts for children eager to read on their own

READING WITH HELP
Engaging stories, longer sentences, and language play for developing readers

READING ALONE
Complex plots, challenging vocabulary, and high-interest topics for the independent reader

ADVANCED READING
Short paragraphs, chapters, and exciting themes for the perfect bridge to chapter books

I Can Read Books have introduced children to the joy of reading since 1957. Featuring award-winning authors and illustrators and a fabulous cast of beloved characters, I Can Read Books set the standard for beginning readers.

A lifetime of discovery begins with the magical words **"I Can Read!"**

Visit www.icanread.com for information
on enriching your child's reading experience.

For Jennifer and Jay Thompson,
with love
—P.P.

For Peggy
—L.S.

HarperCollins®, ♣®, and I Can Read Book® are trademarks of HarperCollins Publishers.

Library of Congress Cataloging-in-Publication Data

Parish, Peggy.
  Amelia Bedelia and the baby / Peggy Parish ; pictures by Lynn Sweat.
    p. cm.—(An I can read book)
  Summary: Amelia Bedelia follows to the letter the list of instructions for looking after the Lanes' baby.
  ISBN-10: 0-688-00316-8 (trade bdg.) — ISBN-13: 978-0-688-00316-6 (trade bdg.)
  ISBN-10: 0-688-00321-4 (lib. bdg.) — ISBN-13: 978-0-688-00321-0 (lib. bdg.)
  ISBN-10: 0-06-051105-2 (pbk.) — ISBN-13: 978-0-06-051105-0 (pbk.)
  [1. Baby sitters—Fiction. 2. Humorous stories.] I. Sweat, Lynn, ill. II. Title.
PZ7.P219 Amm   80-22263
[E]   CIP
                                                                AC

Originally published by Greenwillow Books, an imprint of HarperCollins Publishers, in 1981.

I Can Read!

READING 2 WITH HELP

Amelia Bedelia and the Baby

by Peggy Parish
pictures by Lynn Sweat

HarperCollins*Publishers*

"But Mrs. Rogers,"

said Amelia Bedelia.

"I don't know a thing about babies.

How can I babysit?"

"Why, Amelia Bedelia!"

said Mrs. Rogers.

"You are very good with children."

"Yes," said Amelia Bedelia.

"I get along fine with children."

"Babies are children, too,"

said Mrs. Rogers.

"If you say so,"

said Amelia Bedelia.

"Now you run along,"

said Mrs. Rogers.

"Mrs. Lane is waiting."

So Amelia Bedelia ran

to Mrs. Lane's house.

She knocked on the door.

"Do come in," said Mrs. Lane.

"I'm already late."

8

"Here is your list.

I hope I didn't forget anything.

But you will know what to do."

"I will?" said Amelia Bedelia.

"I gave Missy her lunch,"

said Mrs. Lane.

"She is in her playpen."

Mrs. Lane left.

"How about that?"

said Amelia Bedelia.

"Babies are kept in pens."

Amelia Bedelia found Missy.

"Hi, Missy," she said.

Missy looked at Amelia Bedelia.

She began to cry.

"Oh, oh," said Amelia Bedelia.

"What should I do?

What does the list say?"

11

Amelia Bedelia read,

"Give Missy a bottle."

She hurried to the kitchen.

Then she stopped.

"That can't be right,"

said Amelia Bedelia.

"Babies shouldn't have bottles.

They could break."

She thought a bit.

"I know," she said.

"I'll give her a can

or maybe a box."

Missy howled louder.

"I'll give her both,"

said Amelia Bedelia.

And she did.

Missy picked up the can.

She threw it.

She picked up the box.

She threw it.

And she howled.

"All right," said Amelia Bedelia.

"I'll find something else."

She gave Missy one thing

after another.

But Missy just howled louder.

16

"Maybe you are hungry,"
said Amelia Bedelia.
"I'll get you a cookie."
She ran to the kitchen.
The back door opened.
"Anybody home?"
called Mrs. Carter.

"I'm here," said Amelia Bedelia.

"Here are some strawberries,"
said Mrs. Carter.

"I hear Missy.
Why is she crying?"

"Beats me," said Amelia Bedelia.
"I'm at my wit's end."

"Have you given her a bottle?"
said Mrs. Carter.

"A bottle!" said Amelia Bedelia.
"I have not."

"I think that is what
she wants," said Mrs. Carter.
"I will fix one for her.
You put the strawberries
in something else.
I need my basket."
"All right," said Amelia Bedelia.

Soon Mrs. Carter said,

"The bottle is ready."

"Good," said Amelia Bedelia.

"Here is your basket."

Mrs. Carter left.

Amelia Bedelia looked at the bottle.

"Always something new," she said.

"This bottle won't break.

It's just fine for babies."

She gave the bottle to Missy.

Missy stopped crying.

"I am glad to know
about those bottles,"
said Amelia Bedelia.

"They do shush up babies."

Missy finished her bottle.

Amelia Bedelia looked at the list.

"Good," she said.

"You get a bath now.

I know about that."

Amelia Bedelia got everything ready.

She put Missy in the tub.

Soon Missy was all clean.

"That's done," said Amelia Bedelia.

"Back into your pen you go."

Amelia Bedelia got the list.

She read, "Be sure

to use the baby powder."

She found the powder.

And Amelia Bedelia used it.

"My, I smell good," she said.

"That was nice of Mrs. Lane.

Now what does she want me to do?"

She looked at the list.

"From two until three

is nap time," said Amelia Bedelia.

She shook her head.

"No!" said Amelia Bedelia.

"I won't do it.

I won't take a nap. I hate naps!"

Amelia Bedelia thought a bit.

Then she said, "I know!

Those strawberries!

I will make a surprise.

I do make good strawberry tarts."

She started for the kitchen.

"First," she said,

"I'll see what Missy is doing."

She went to the playpen.

"How about that!

Missy likes naps,"

said Amelia Bedelia.

"She can take mine for me.

I've got better things to do."

31

She went to the kitchen.
She put some of this
and a little of that
into a bowl.

She mixed and mixed.

Soon her tarts were made.

"Those do look pretty,"

she said.

She put the tarts away.

Missy began to cry.

"Missy is awake,"

said Amelia Bedelia.

"Let me see what

I should do."

"It says to give her

a mashed banana," she said.

"That will be easy."

She got a banana.

And she mashed it.

"This is fun," said Amelia Bedelia.

"But I better give it to Missy."

Missy took the banana.

She looked at it.

Then she mashed it.

She mashed it harder and harder.

Suddenly the skin popped.

Banana squished all over Missy.

Missy clapped her hands.

Then she ate the squishy banana.

Amelia Bedelia laughed.

"I never saw anything

like that before," she said.

"But she had fun.

And it was her banana."

Then Missy began to fuss.

"I can forget the list for now,"

said Amelia Bedelia.

"I know what you need.

You need another bath."

So Missy got another bath.

"Babies do need a lot of washing,"

said Amelia Bedelia.

She dressed Missy.

"Now back to the list," she said.

"Put Missy
in her stroller,"
she read.
Amelia Bedelia
did that.
Then she read,
"But first, put a sweater on her."

Amelia Bedelia
took Missy
out of the stroller.
"Your mama should
have said that first,"
said Amelia Bedelia.

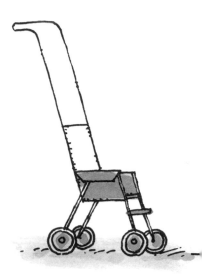

She put a sweater on Missy.
"Back in you go," she said.

She looked at the list again.

"Tarnation!" she said.

"Your mama can't make up

her mind. Now she says

to take you out for a while."

Amelia Bedelia took Missy

out of the stroller.

"In and out. In and out,"

she said. "I'm plumb tired."

Amelia Bedelia put Missy
in her playpen.

She looked at the list.

"You must be out for good,"
she said.

"It says playtime is
until five o'clock.
Now that is a treat.
I don't get to play much."
Amelia Bedelia looked around.
"Now what shall I play?"
she said.
She saw Missy's toy box.
"Look at all the toys!"
she said.

Amelia Bedelia sat down.

She began to play.

She played first with one toy.

Then she played with another.

"Oh, what fun!" she said.

"I wish I had toys like these."

Missy began to fuss.

Amelia Bedelia looked

at her watch.

"Shoot!" she said.

"It's five o'clock.

Playtime is over."

She put away the toys.

Then she looked at the list.

"It's time for your supper,"

she said.

"The list says I should give you

some baby food."

Amelia Bedelia picked up Missy.

They went to the kitchen.

Amelia Bedelia put Missy

in her chair.

She took off Missy's sweater
and then read from the list,
"Don't forget
to put on Missy's bib."
Amelia Bedelia found the bib.
"That's plumb cute," she said.
And Amelia Bedelia put it on.

"Now," she said,

"I'll make your supper."

Amelia Bedelia scurried around.

She made baby hamburgers.

She cooked baby potatoes.

She sliced baby tomatoes.

"That is a good supper,"
said Amelia Bedelia.
She started to give it to Missy.
"Oh, oh," she said. "The catsup.
I forgot the catsup."
She poured catsup
over everything.
"Children do love catsup,"
said Amelia Bedelia.
She gave Missy her supper.
Missy tasted it. She smiled.
And Missy ate her supper.

Amelia Bedelia laughed.

"You really liked that," she said.

"You will like this, too."

Amelia Bedelia got a strawberry tart.

"Here," she said.

Missy grabbed the tart.

She ate all of that, too.

"You are a mess,"

said Amelia Bedelia.

"You need washing again."

Mr. and Mrs. Lane came in.

"My baby!" said Mrs. Lane.

"What did you do to her?

What is that red stuff?"

"Red stuff?" said Amelia Bedelia.

"Oh, some of it is catsup,"
she said.

"The rest is strawberries."

"Catsup! Strawberries!"
said Mrs. Lane.

"She can't eat things like that."

"Oh, yes she can,"

said Amelia Bedelia.

"She loves them."

"Why did I leave Missy with you!"

said Mrs. Lane.

"You don't know a thing

about babies."

Mr. Lane ate a strawberry tart.

"Delicious," he said.

"Don't you ever—"

said Mrs. Lane.

But that was as far as she got.

Her mouth was full

of strawberry tart.

"My favorite!" she said.

Missy began to cry.

Mrs. Lane went to her.

But Missy wanted Amelia Bedelia.

"She never did that before,"

said Mr. Lane.

"Amelia Bedelia must know

something we don't."

"I think she knows a lot,"

said Mrs. Lane.

"I'm sorry I got angry.

Will you come again?"

"I would love to,"

said Amelia Bedelia.

"But I have to go now."

Amelia Bedelia walked home.

"I declare," she said.

"That was plumb fun.

Babies are real people.

And I get along

just fine with them."